STORIES FROM THE FLOOD
LISMORE, AUSTRALIA

COMPILED BY YAGIA GENTLE

INTRODUCTION BY DR AIDAN RICKETS

ASSISTED BY MICK MARGAN

"There is a tide in the affairs of men,

Which, taken at the flood, leads on to fortune.

Omitted, all the voyage of their life

is bound in shallows and in miseries."

Shakespeare

(Romeo and Juliet)

Dedicated to the brave and selfless people who saw what needed to be done, and did it.

eBook ISBN: 979-8-89795-809-2
Paperback ISBN: 979-8-89795-810-8
Hardcover ISBN: 979-8-89795-811-5

Lismore, NSW, Australia, February, 2024

Correspondence to *yagiagentle@gmail.com*

CONTENTS

PROLOGUE

This book is a collection of interviews for the local Nimbin Good Times newspaper, which were published through 2023.

The floods of February 2022 were devastating for the whole Northern Rivers NSW community. Everyone has been affected. Blame for it spreads like oil on water. As it disperses, no one thing stands out. Climate change, the undersea earthquake near Tonga two weeks earlier, deforestation, the chance combination of weather events, or, as the local Aboriginal people warned, "It's a meeting of two rivers, it's always flooded here".

The water level exceeded 14 metres, creating the most expensive disaster in Australia's history, and the second most expensive in the world at the time. Twenty people died, many were injured, and thousands lost their homes and businesses. The insurance council puts the economic cost at about 6 billion dollars, but many people were not insured.

For some, it was a temporary inconvenience, no shops, no internet, no services, and no power for a while, while for others it was a matter of survival, followed by post-traumatic stress disorder. Hanging on to the gutter of your house for hours in a raging, freezing torrent of water after escaping through a broken window is not easy to come down from emotionally. Having your dad drown, or your house and business destroyed, and leaving you homeless is akin to surviving a war zone. Yet this is what people went through. Trauma works as a coping mechanism for living through a frightening experience. The fight or flight hormones work overtime, and after the threat has passed, cortisol runs through the blood for a while in case the threat hasn't gone away, meaning it doesn't take much to trigger the adrenaline to start again. Triggering the person to have a rapid heartbeat, tense muscles, short emotional tolerance, low digestive capacity, and sleep disorder. Now, when the rain comes, as it does often in the sub tropics of this area, many people are triggered. It takes time, safety, compassion, and community for this to change and heal.

The people we interviewed were happy to tell their stories. They allowed us to have a mere glimpse of what they went through, and are sometimes still going through. The interviews began when I went to see Satnam as an emergency student counsellor. I was shocked by how he stoically stood alone in the middle of what was his beautiful restaurant. He hadn't yet allowed screams and cries to take over him. We became friends after that, and he afterwards invited me to the Sikh temple and his housewarming. When he got the restaurant running again, I thought of how I could help and wrote his story for the paper. Then my wife suggested I talk with the owners of Daley's shop. The coming together of the stories began, and Nick came to help. We approach people as a counsellor, rather than an interviewer. Allowing the person to say as much as they felt. We talked to people from politicians to mums and dads, trying to see the disaster and the recovery from various angles, various depths, and various ideas of the future.

INTRODUCTION

Dr Aidan Ricketts

Social Change educator

Law lecturer (Southern Cross University)

What can we learn from our stories of disaster?

In 2022, the Northern Rivers experienced a record-smashing flood and landscape collapse. In most accounts of that time, there is plenty of attention on trauma, frustration, government or insurance company failures, or upon the heroics of what must have been one of the largest and most successful civilian rescue efforts in Australia's history.

But beneath all of the hardship and loss lies another story. Reading the stories in this volume and reflecting upon that year, I have been moved to try to accommodate the tragedy with the triumph, the loss with the growth, the beauty with the horror, and to seek to articulate what we have learned about ourselves, about disasters, and about the underestimated power of community.

Somewhere deep in the evolutionary brain of humans is a special capacity for natural disasters. When it is activated, we get to witness some of the most inspirational qualities of humans, both individually and collectively. From the courage and calm of those trapped in or on roofs, to the selfless courage of their rescuers, to the generosity of spirit of entire communities both in and around disaster, to the collective processing of trauma, we have been privileged to witness something truly remarkable.

Beneath the seemingly inexorable drudgery of civilisation, of a world dominated by disembodiment, consumerism and individualism, and the debilitating cult of authority, lies human potentials of immense power, beauty and sheer practical usefulness.

For the vast majority, disaster unleashes what is great within us.

The local community will always be the first responders. This is true not only of rescue (the immediate life-saving) but also of the much longer and more wearying road of recovery.

This is not to criticise the value or role of professional emergency services, but to acknowledge that what we witnessed was not the failure of government, but actually its inherent and unavoidable limits.

It is impossible for the state to have enough boats, personnel, or organising capacity to match what a self-organising community can offer up virtually in an instant. The community lives in and amongst its own disaster, and its resources of all kinds become mobilised almost instantly. From the tinny army, to the many fine people who magically appear at the drop off points to take in soggy refugees to feed and clothe them, to the emergent relief groups such as Helping Hands, Koori Mail and Resilience Lismore, and beyond that to the distributed emergent activities throughout the region, these are our most powerful and effective first responders and always will be.

Government, even emergency services, have organisational models that function well enough in predictable scenarios but are caught out when the domain of chaos calls for instant responses to novel challenges. In the language of complexity theory, in an 'emergency,' the most powerful first response is the 'emergent' one.

What we experienced with the collapse of the police, the overstretch of the SES, and the dysfunction of communications infrastructure was not an aberration; it was exactly what a major disaster looks and feels like, and self-organising and emergent community response will always need to respond to that gap.

American author Rebecca Solnit researched natural disasters around the world for her book aptly titled "A Paradise Built in Hell" and she explored the stories of numerous major disasters around the globe, including Hurricane Katrina, and her recurring insight is that the greatest asset in disaster response is self-organising communities and the greatest single risk is 'elite panic' where authorities or property owners wrongly assume that the community will descend into violence and looting and respond inappropriately with oppressive authoritarian interventions. Thankfully, this kind of over-reach didn't occur in Lismore.

In the many stories of individuals, families, businesses, and how they responded, we can learn so many lessons for future disasters.

Our first lesson, in the first days and weeks, the government will spin its wheels trying to get its large hierarchical, risk-averse structures to mobilise, and the 100% best practice response of government would be to first and foremost resource the community's mobilisation as fully and freely as the bean counters can tolerate. Literally drop a cool few million onto the emergent structures and stop the control fantasy that the community may not spend it as wisely as a room full of bureaucrats (on big wages) might spend it three months down the line.

Someone was already paying for the tinny fuel, the clothes, and the sandwiches, just support them!

Secondly, and I think Lismore did this well, respect the community response, don't inhibit it, don't try to corral it, and don't engage in the authoritarian fantasy that the community will descend into mob chaos without the state. The truth is, the chaos is the terrain already, and the spontaneity of the community is its best antidote.

This brings me to lesson three. Leave your fixed safety mentality at the kerb. This is a disaster, and safety left the building a while ago. Faced with the potential for massive loss of life, each rescuer did what they had to do to reduce the risks that already existed; pure safety was never an option. Faced with a mountain of mud, every volunteer recovery crew did what they had to do and took all of the necessary risks.

The Lismore free state was a place in time where the veneer of society was stripped away, where money was irrelevant, and where goodwill was currency, and it lasted for many weeks. It hibernates, ready for when it is called upon again. Government can never replace this capacity, but it could respect and support it better.

The other great lesson is about that other monolithic governance system of our time, the insurance cartels. Seriously, in my observations, those without flood insurance were better able to retain control of their own disaster journey and their own recovery than many with insurance. I have heard so many harrowing stories of gangs of 'make safe' goons sent by insurance companies, bullying vulnerable people and stripping homes of the wear-and-tear for recovery. Tearing out wooden lining boards, plumbing, and even floors, then leaving. Having completely displaced people from their homes, the insurance companies sometimes decided, you didn't have flood insurance anyway, or if you did, we won't get on to a rebuild for more than a year.

I am not saying mistakes were not made by well-wishing volunteers partaking in recovery; we know the orgy of disposal became somewhat irrational and harmful at times, but it's nothing on the scale of the impact of the insurance company's reckless interventions.

There is another whole story to be told of how post-disaster processes such as property buy-outs and flood rebuilding grants should be administered, but it is well beyond the scope of this publication.

The stories in this book are just a few of the thousands of similar but different accounts of the human spirit, generosity in adversity, and collective cooperation. As a disaster community, we can be rightly proud of ourselves; we are an inspiration to many, and as the escalating chaos of climate change engulfs Australia and the world, our learnings and our collective and individual growth and wisdom will be a resource for survival for many communities in the future.

All the best to our great community as we continue to grow from our disastrous emergency, thanks for emerging. For all who read these stories, never forget the power of community, and we will all meet again next time we are needed.

CHAPTER 1
ELLIE BIRD

My disaster story really started back after the 2017 flood, when I was part of an incredible group of individuals who responded to that event as 'Lismore Helping Hands'. We ran a flood centre for about 3 weeks. Then, between 2017 and 2022, I did a lot of resilience work both at the community level and in trying to do what I could as a Councillor on Lismore City Council to get us in a better shape as far as disaster planning goes. That was a really difficult thing to try to achieve. Council went through a lot of upheaval at that time, and it was hard to keep recovery planning on the agenda.

I kind of always knew that one day a big flood would happen because I focused on learning about floods and about disasters after 2017, but like everybody else, I was totally caught by surprise by how big the February 2022 flood was. As that flood hit us, a group of the same people from 2017 stood up again immediately, and ever since then, I haven't really stopped. I do big weeks and big hours, coordinating our community-based flood recovery work. I work with an incredible and dedicated group of people doing whatever we can to look after people in our community, and there's still so much more we need to do.

We changed our name to Resilient Lismore, and we started with the immediate need of cleaning out homes and managing donations. There were lots of community initiatives doing that work, because there was so much to do. We started organising a range of community support, and we became a fairly central community initiative in the recovery.   I think from the time of the flood, I've been doing something like 60-hour weeks. I administer a fairly large Facebook group, 'Resilient Lismore – Community Recovery and Resilience,' and as the emergency started to escalate, a team of us were doing what we could to amplify and share information. A couple of days after we started to build our organising systems, which use various internet platforms to organise work and help people. We moved down to the CBD and worked out of an undercover car park opposite the library. We were there for eight months. Distributing cleaning products, mould cleaner, organising and sending out volunteers, distributing donations, and working with other groups to distribute furniture and other things.

In the initial response, we were managing about 60 people. Coordinating, communicating, and organising, and that was just the administration. We've coordinated thousands of volunteers. We still run a tool library so people can come and borrow things that they need to work on their homes, and we run a couple of projects. We run the two rooms project, where we coordinate volunteers to go out and build walls, and we recently entered into a partnership with the Reece Foundation around restoring bathrooms and toilets, and essential plumbing. We're just working as fast as we can to scale that work up and keep helping the people who need our help. And there's still a lot of them. We don't just work in Lismore, we work in surrounding communities as well. We work downstream in places like Wardell, Woodburn, and Coraki, where they've been hit badly too.

Many other community initiatives haven't been able to maintain their efforts using volunteers, or haven't managed to get funding, whereas we have; we've managed to sustain ourselves so we can keep helping our community.

Because we had our experience from 2017, we knew how long this recovery would take, and we knew how important it is for a community-based initiative to be here for the long term. That's why it was so important from early on that we focused on stabilising our funding model so that we can continue to be an effective, functioning entity. We didn't want to burn out. In the 2017 flood recovery, we ran with 100% volunteers, and we just ran out of puff. It's not sustainable that way, so we made sure that we put in grant applications, and we have been successful in receiving some grant funding through Healthy North Coast, Department of Community and Justice, Northern Rivers Community Foundation, and various other philanthropic organisations. That funding is keeping us going.

Resilient Lismore has now evolved to a point where we are

helping people rebuild their homes, which we call a 'Repair to Return 'model. We are helping people by making sure that they have some walls in the house so they've got somewhere where they can keep warm, we try to make sure people have a working toilet, and we are starting to repair bathrooms and kitchens.

We operate now from the old Trevan Ford showroom on Keen Street, four days a week, and we are still very busy here helping people with donations. At the moment, we are surrounded by blankets and stuff because it's winter. We do a lot of donations. Personally, I've also done quite a bit of advocacy since the floods. I sit on various committees and talk to a lot of bureaucrats about what our community needs. I try to share data and information about what we're seeing on the ground with the people we are working with. I'm also on the Lismore City Council, so I navigate those processes and challenges as well.

Disaster Recovery is a very complicated landscape. It can get very confusing. There are disaster recovery arrangements in place, which involve the state and federal government sharing the cost of disaster recovery programs. There's a number of bureaucracies, including a reasonably new one at the Federal level called the National Emergency Management Authority. Then there's the newly established Reconstruction Authority of New South Wales and the Northern Rivers Reconstruction Corporation. It is incredibly complex and complicated, and how it all intersects with the council is another layer of complexity.

The recovery committees and structures are state government committees. Council staff often participate in those processes, particularly around infrastructure. Council hosts some staff who are engaged in the recovery committee process, and councillors themselves are engaged at a strategic level with getting updates and information from the Reconstruction Corporation wherever possible, and getting feedback through those forums, which isn't an easy process, and it's often frustrating.

I think we have a really long way to go as a community. We have a lot of thinking to do, a lot of conversations to have about how we live in a place that has such a high risk, and is still recovering from one of the worst disasters Australia has ever seen.

I think as it moves into history and becomes something that is more in the past, it's important that we remember the significance of what's happened here. We have a long way to go, not just in terms of repairing people's homes so that they can live somewhere with dignity, but also in terms of how we exist as a city that lives right on the riverbank in a place that is such a high-risk, one of the highest-risk places in Australia. We have to have some big conversations together to work out how we manage that risk.

How do we retain our vibrancy and the things that make this place such a special part of the world? I think we just have to keep talking to each other. And we have to move through the hard bits with compassion for each other and for everyone else that's in the landscape. As a community, we are incredibly frustrated at the moment, and rightly so, because it's a huge recovery and we have so many layers of bureaucracy to navigate and a tangled government response. It's very easy to get angry about how that's all playing out, but for me, it's important to come back to the value, the strength, and the benefit that we have in being a community that is relatively well-connected. We have to look after each other as we move through that, and we have to have brave, courageous, and honest conversations with each other.

Structurally, it's going to be interesting to see what happens as the Northern Rivers Reconstruction Corporation rolls up with the

NSW Reconstruction Authority and how that will influence what is happening at the State level. Apparently, there is a community engagement process starting soon, which will be a significant process, so I'm hopeful that that's going to be a space where we can have the big conversations we need to have about what our future looks like here on the floodplain.

I often say here at Resilient Lismore that it's a big life. I think that sums it up well enough. It's a big life, and often it's a really hard life, and if I know anything, it's that here in this community, we know that.

CHAPTER 2
SOUTHERN CROSS UNIVERSITY
BEN ROACH

I guess I should start with my role at the uni. I'm a part of the executive team. My job is with the external engagement of the university. That is, engaging with positive change outside of the university.

In the period leading up to the flood, everyone had been working and studying from home in those incredibly bizarre Covid years, and we were really excited to be welcoming staff and students physically back to the campus. Instead, we had to completely close. It poured on that Sunday, and on Monday morning, we woke to a crisis. After experiencing the 2017 flood, I had a sense of what would be coming. Then we had by far the biggest flood in the region's history.

We had a meeting of our governing body scheduled in Coffs Harbour for that Monday, so we had a situation where the Vice Chancellor and some of the executive team were there preparing for it. Then of course the highway closed, and they were stranded, so I found myself as the first member of the executive team to be on campus, and then I was given the authority to manage the whole response. It was very challenging; the work was seven days a week for six months. It was a furious amount of work. I had to figure out what's required, what services we have that we could put into place, and what we can do for the community. The uni caters to almost 18,000 people. About half of our staff and students are local and would be impacted, so we had a duty of care around how we support them as well.

After the 2017 flood, I recognised how little had been learnt from that event by the government. The preparation plans had not been enacted. I was shocked at the incompetence. But my anger motivated me to do it properly. I felt a real sense of obligation. I've lived here for 14 years and feel I'm deeply connected; I even helped build a new school in town. All of that was lost. I felt deeply concerned about the ability of our town to recover.

It was in those days that we saw a huge number of staff, students, and volunteers from the community descend on the campus. It was just remarkable. That sense of community spirit was in the tinny army. The university has some boats used for research. I said, "We have to get every available boat in the water". We had professors, cleaners, and everyone was out there helping the tinny army.

The sense of responsibility was overarching for me. I was conscious of the fact that the university had an opportunity to deliver a level of care that it had never delivered before. I remember that evening walking down to the campus car park in a complete blackout, and there were people starting to set up tents on any green patch they could find. They were around campfires, trying to dry gear. It was remarkable. It felt a little bit like I'm sure many would've felt in New Orleans, post-hurricane Katrina. It felt that the fabric of civilisation itself was torn a little bit, and I have to say that sensation grew over the next few days, because we had deeply traumatised and vulnerable people arriving, either finding their way over land, or literally coming out of the air by helicopter drops from the Australian Defence Force. They would arrive in traumatised groups, sometimes 50 people at a time. There was no coordination then; we didn't know they were coming. And over time, it swelled to 3 or 4,000 people. We were opening up classrooms, trying to give them some sense of sheltered safety, although we were completely unprepared.

The scale of trauma from this event was quite confronting. Often, the staff or volunteers were the ones to greet people arriving from the helicopters or the boats. They were disoriented. Many were catatonic. Many were unable to speak; they were in such deep shock and trauma.

Up to then, the concept of values was academic. Then they became the basis for our decisions, and our academic training gave us the ability to act for them. This experience forced us to rethink the strategy of the university towards being an organisation that changes people's lives.

We arranged food to go back into the communities and the villages. In those days, after the flood, no one was receiving donations. No one was even able to receive donations. We were also aware that there was no food, especially fresh food, so we set up distribution networks to get food into villages and communities.

We set up a food and clothing system so that we could get dry clothing into the communities, and we started to see ourselves as a hub, not only for safety, but also for distribution and regeneration. I remember one Saturday, I got a phone call at about 6 am. It was a really well-intentioned truck driver who was driving a semi-trailer from the Harris farm markets in Sydney. A donation of 22 pallets of fresh fruit and vegetables. At that stage, we hadn't seen fresh food for weeks. The man said it will arrive at ten o'clock, and we have to unload and store it. We put out a call on Facebook and all the media sites. People started turning up and getting the word out. Communities like Cabbage Tree Island, Woodburn, Whyralla, and Coraki had really suffered and been overlooked by the services. They started to feel supported.

As we were unloading the truck, my 11-year-old son said to me, "Dad, there's people crying when they take their first bite of a plum." It was pretty emotional.

That was the kind of community building that we suddenly found ourselves in, and that became self-sustaining. I think most people derived great motivation, and I think joy, from the help that they could provide. So many people involved in the mud clean-ups and helping strangers found purpose in their lives over that time.

In the weeks after, we had two police stations on campus. The ambulance station was operating out of here. The fire station was here. The town had no financial or banking system for a while until we created one in the plaza. The whole emergency response operation was based on the second level of this building. And of course, there was the evacuation centre, with all its complexities. So we found ourselves right in the centre of it all, and not really by choice, but by moral obligation. Then we had to strategize around what recovery looks like.

I wasn't personally affected by the floodwater, and I think it's an important part of the story, because I was able to bring my whole self to work. My circumstances allowed me to invest fully in the work. I remember on the second day, I gathered the university leadership group together and had a short discussion. We agreed that we need to say 'Yes' to anything and figure it out later. That was how we took on the evacuation centre, and accommodation of TAFE, Richmond River High, The Living School, and Trinity School. I maintained the lead in terms of the external interface into the university, and my colleague Alan Morris ran the internal operations. I would find the need, and then give it to Alan to implement.

The scale was huge. There was so much happening. We had all of those services happening, and we were aware that the business community was struggling to function. How would people get paid?

We needed to create a banking system, as well as a business recovery system. Then there was the health service. Not a single medical centre was operating in Lismore, and there was, and still is, a huge level of trauma. So by the third week, we worked with the primary health network to set up Head to Health, a mental health service. Then there was also another response we needed to look at. We were concerned about the level of resilience of young people in the region.

I think the response to COVID has been pretty disproportionate and has been particularly difficult on high school kids. Then, to see that slam into the flood event, we got really concerned. We felt a deep sense of obligation to try to hold the kids and the education system together. After the flood, many schools were unable to operate, so I went out of my way to contact all of the leads of all of those schools and said, "We are here for you, and will do whatever you need," and I mean that. We helped relocate the schools on our land; we've still got them all here, two years later.

Now we're starting to think about, well, what all of that looks like for our region going forward. How do we build a much better education system that is stronger and better able to support the kind of potential that we have here in our region?

Very quickly, I realised that we can't go back into a scenario where people face this kind of risk. I'm not saying that we shouldn't allow people to have a choice. I think we shouldn't have a housing system that results in the most vulnerable living in the most dangerous parts of our community. In the recovery, we've got every opportunity to change that, and every minute that I invest in this flood recovery is focused on ensuring that we do not repeat the same mistakes of the past over and over again.

Our role is to help equip the organisations that are going to be tasked with the rebuild and the recovery process to make better choices, and this calls for a dedicated reconstruction authority. When the flood hit, we had a bunch of state government agencies that were absent and useless, and they've been trying to catch up ever since. I'm still concerned about their ability to make decisions based on the lived experience of our community, and other communities that have faced similar disasters, like Christchurch, Louisiana, the Pacific islands, there are so many examples. We need to draw on all the innovations, ideas, and expertise available. Grantham, in Queensland, is an example. They moved the whole town! Lots of risk. Lots of people are saying it's too expensive. A disproportionate response, etc. But it worked. And that came out of the mayor and a few people discussing big ideas.

We have to get things right this time. I realised we have to reach out. So we developed the 'Northern Rivers Living Lab'. The expertise in recovery from disasters is scattered over the world, so we have been bringing it under one network that can provide support for those complex choices that communities and governments are going to have to make.

The bit that's available to the public is our shop front on 11 Woodlark Street. We set it up so that we can have informal conversations with the public around housing. What types of housing exist, and what does density look like in other countries? I don't think we've seen great examples in Australia of really innovative housing solutions. There are really great examples all around the world, so we want to bring those ideas to the community here, to say, "Look, there are heaps of ideas. Don't think that housing density equals skyscrapers. It can also be sustainable, regenerative, and provide great social connectedness". We're not trying to put a solution forward. We're at the stage of supporting conversation with good information.

So the uni has gotten to a stage now where the journey has moved on from being personal and individualistic, to an obligation to our community. It's kind of emblematic of the flood experience. That started as an intensely personal step into a harrowing experience, and is merging into a system to help a community that works together. We naturally reacted to the flood by building a broader community-based response. Now we're moving into a more contemplative state, and I see the role of the university now is to continue to be that platform for community support and change. Indeed, if the community needs something, come and ask, and we'll work out how we can be supportive.

We are big enough that the government will listen, yet small enough to listen to our community. People can walk into the Living Lab shopfront and feel safe, because it's not the government, and it's not all these big agencies in uniform. It's a genuine community space.

How do we build genuine resilience and adaptation such that we come back from this flood event in a way where it's not just building back better, but we respond to these opportunities around deep resilience, regeneration, and adaptation? This is the opportunity we've got to seize.

That care-based response really changed how we think about ourselves as a university. It's a profound element of institutional change, and we became a different kind of university as a result. When we all got together afterwards, we realised some of our care stepped out of normal boundaries. Like seeing people going through the agony of drug withdrawal and organising a methadone bus for them on a Saturday morning. Gosh, we didn't even question it at the time, because we knew it needed to be done.

Now my view on universities has become really simple. We are public institutions with a societal purpose, and this is the time to express that intent.

CHAPTER 3
DALEY'S HOMEWARES AND UNIFORMS MATHEW AND JANE.

❖

Jane

It was my husband's birthday the day of the first flood. We thought we were prepared. Mathew put everything up, and then the devastation hit. Nobody was really prepared. Mathew, my brother, stayed in the shop. I stayed home, in Alstonville, managing his anxiety over the phone and posting his pictures on social media because I knew that other businesses wanted to know what was happening. It was absolute, utter devastation everywhere. We kept thinking that there were people around who needed help.

When the water receded, we came back to town for the clean-up. I couldn't bring myself to throw everything into the landfill. We had staff, family, established customers, and even strangers, taking anything possible to wash. At least twenty washing machines were operating at any one time. It was incredible the way passing strangers would come to help, and even take soiled stock home and bring it back looking new. Those same people would then purchase stuff to give to flood victims. Our shop evolved to become a central point for distributing food and blankets. The only way we were fed was through people donating food, and then we would go over and support the rescue centers. We were all helping each other. It was extraordinary.

We had the first big flood, and then after three weeks, we had to pack again for the second flood. We lost everything. Like everybody in Lismore, we had no flood insurance. We had to rely on our suppliers for extended credit and selling stock that we had managed to salvage. Over the years, we have donated and supplied lots of organisations with bedding and bathroom ware, and they supported us. Some of our suppliers gave us good discounts, which we passed on.

The community has just been amazing, how it's rallied together. The quantity of donations, the practical and emotional support that's been given. Lots of people have bought gift vouchers from us for flood victims. It's a win-win that's helped keep us afloat, and people came from all over Australia to help in the disaster. Some would buy a gift from our shop, and that was a big help. Actually, the hardest thing in our recovery has been the council closing Keen St for renovations. That's another story. The council got a grant to fix the footpath, and the work was extended to six months because of different issues they had. We missed out on the Christmas trade and foot traffic. That really set back our return to business.

Now we're taking it one day at a time. I don't get traumatised when I hear the sound of rain, like many of the people who experienced the flood, but I do get emotional when I talk about it. I try to live for the present and the future, not for the past.

Mathew

Daleys was started in 1989 by my cousin. We started in Molesworth Street, then in Woodlark, and we've been in Keen St for nearly nineteen years. In the flood, the water came halfway up the window of the second floor. We lost everything. All up, it has cost me about $300,000. We got a tiny portion of assistance from the government, so we just had to suck it up, dust ourselves off, and see if we could trade our way out.

We have a well thought out flood plan, sleeping in the shop, and moving everything up to the top floor. But this flood was different. I was woken at 4 in the morning, the water breached the levee and roared through town. An absolute torrent. Ripping off doors and sending big rubbish skips down the street. We had a big steel counter in the shop that floated away. I don't know where it went. The water kept rising and rising and getting louder. I kept moving stock up, but the water got to everything. When it started to recede, I followed it, hosing the mud off the walls. I know that if the mud sets, it's difficult to clean. All the established businesses in town know what to do in a flood, but this one was so big that it got to the plaster ceiling, where all the infrastructure is held. The air conditioning, lights, data cables, etc. When the ceiling collapsed, it all came down. We're still not fully recovered from that.

So after the flood, it took us a couple of days to take stock. We decided to try to recover what we could, rather than throw it away, and work on fixing up the shop. We had strangers and customers washing stuff for us. We were constantly getting help from the community. It was just astonishing. We knew that this place had a big heart, but to actually see it first-hand, it was so humbling. What really got me was the rallying around afterwards, when people made an effort to come to town and support the businesses that had reopened. We're the ones who support the netball and soccer teams. We're the ones who support the local kids. The big chains don't sponsor community events. There's no K-mart netball club, but there's a Daleys netball club. The community knows this, and they have been supporting the small, local businesses. Now it's a year after the flood and we've had to re-imagine our business into a manchester, homewares and uniform business. It's slowly picking up. Lismore is slowly waking up from the beating. It will take us years to fully recover, and it will be different than before, but Lismore will be back, and once again be the pulsing heart of the Northern Rivers.

CHAPTER 4
LISMORE LIBRARY
LUCY AND MICHAEL

Lucy

We were down there Sunday afternoon, madly packing up. Everything on the ground floor was on wheels, so we could just move it upstairs in the lift. We walked away thinking we were safe.

At one o'clock the next morning, I got a phone call from a staff member who lived across from the library. He rang up and said, 'It's on the middle floor', and I knew everything was gone.

That staff member was asking to go into the library to get away from his apartment. He was on the roof at the time. He got rescued by a boat, like so many people.

We knew that the library would be needed in the community after such a big disaster. So we opened up a little branch library in the Goonellabah industrial estate, put more books down at Goonellabah library, and went from there.

The mobile library trailer (which goes to Nimbin) was in floodwater, so it was damaged as well. Unfortunately, the part that was in the water was all the electronics, so the insurance company wrote it off.

In the meantime, our staff ran the service with boxes out of a station wagon. They'd unload the books onto trestle tables at each stop, pack up again, every day for six days a week. Often in the pouring rain.

After some months, we were able to source a second-hand trailer. It was in Melbourne, and they actually drove it up for free because of what had happened. A lot of places gave things that aren't physically visible, but they were all affected by the library being flooded.

The donations started coming in early on, from all over Australia. Soon, we were literally getting palettes of books being delivered. Kennards across the road, very generously, would send their little forklift over and unload them for us.

Anyone and everyone was sending them. Unknown people, organisations, publishers, libraries, schools. Anyone. That image of the library books outside the library had such an impact across Australia.

We were contacted by a charity in Victoria called 123Read2Me. They collect children's books and give them to people who need them. They have sent seven pallet-loads of children's books, each containing about 600 kilograms of books.

We've been able to distribute them to the YWCA, to patrons at our libraries, the Merry Markets, NAIDOC week over at the turf club, and the lantern parade. Giving away books helped us provide the feeling that Lismore is a happy space. We're still doing it.

We received a substantial amount of financial help from the community across Australia, but the fact that many of the books in our libraries are donated books is special. I think that has more impact than if we'd spent a thousand dollars buying them. They would have just been normal books, but these are community books.

Libraries are about more than just books; we're also a community hub. We develop relationships with people and provide services like internet, printing, helping people fill out forms, tech lessons, and programs for kids.

One of the things we did was set up the book swap down at Lismore Central. At that stage, there was nothing downtown. The manager of the center said "Yes, you can set up some shelves". It got such a response and such a demand that it is now set up in a whole shop of its own in Lismore Central, multiple shelves, open all the time. I still can't keep up with the shelving!

They set up a Facebook group to share and review the books they'd taken from there. The public set that up themselves. The books are taken there by us, but that's it. It has a life of its own. People go there to have an interaction, and the books help them do that.

The community is not going to be back to normal for years. But the library will be back up and running, better than ever. The light's there and we're heading towards it. We had a flood plan; now we'll just do a new flood plan. We'll work it out. It'll be bigger and better and brighter than ever.

Michael

I hate the BOM radar now because I woke in the middle of the night, looked at the radar, and thought, 'Oh my god, what is this? Just go away!'

I live out of town on a hill. We had a landslide that affected the foundations of our house. But the big thing for me was that a friend of mine was rescued from South Lismore, and he and his family stayed with us.

There was a lot of uncertainty in those first few days. News that a building was on fire was circulating, and he was stressed that it was his property. It was so difficult to tell what was what.

On Wednesday, we finally got into town. He had a small garden, he had chickens, and he had guinea pigs. We got there and we made a makeshift bridge from wood from the timber yard nearby. The chickens, most of them were sitting on the porch, and then he heard the guinea pig squeaking inside, and I just remember him lying down and crying.

It's a small story, but I think there are people who've been impacted, and then there's everyone else who has been impacted around that. There were conversations about guilt, trauma, and things like that. I look at our landslip and the damage to our property, and I think I kinda feel better that it happened because I was a part of it. But eighteen months and $70,000 later, I'm kinda going, 'Uh, I would be fine if that had not happened.'

When I walked into the library after the flood, there was no carpet; it was just books. It was dark, it was gloomy, it stank. It was your work, your community impact, everything was just on the floor in ruins.

The image of the books out the window had an impact. People

would come to us who wanted to give, to share, to talk, to connect. There would be days when you would have someone donating who's crying, and you've got a staff member who's crying. It was cathartic.

The act of giving was supporting people to give them some power over something they felt so powerless over.

In Singapore, there's an international school, and its faculty got a hold of the image, and their community ended up donating five thousand dollars, which went to the flood appeal.

We had over one hundred thousand books donated, and the library lost twenty-nine thousand. All of the donations went into three forty-foot shipping containers and a storage shed here, and Lucy's garage at home, which is large. Thirty-two thousand books have now been digitally catalogued into our system.

There are a few free, open spaces that are available for anyone in the community to come in and learn and connect, and when your home and your library have been wrecked, where do people go?

Libraries have been an open door for people to better themselves and establish themselves. People go to the library to find pathways to better themselves. We pushed to bring our services back with that in mind.

We did a lot of things. One of them was a fines amnesty. People would come in and say, 'Oh, I wasn't able to save the library book.' We were like, 'Forget the library books, you're okay, let's get rid of the charges, don't even think about it. What would you like to borrow today?'

One of the most effective programs has been the social circle, which was established purely to combat social isolation. When I ask people why they come to that, they say, 'I just needed to connect.'

Here we are, eighteen months down the track, and we've done a lot, but we're still hindered by the lack of large, open spaces for community groups to get together. The pop-up library in Lismore is a shop space catering to a population of forty thousand. You have Storytime going on while people are trying to study.

So the next thing we'll do is establish a children's library for children to be children in the library. That will free up the adult space so people can do things like study and better themselves in a better environment.

It's been impossible for me to separate the personal from the professional. At times I thought, 'God, it's an absolute mess.' Other times, I look at how our staff have come together and done this amazing service in the face of such adversity, purely to give their community that connection, and there's a really positive feeling.

We've got a couple of folders full of letters that came with the donations, and what I would like to see is a display in the Lismore library when we get back. I don't think we could just name a couple of people because it was an amazing, collective response.

CHAPTER 5
ANDIE AND NICK,
SOUTH LISMORE

Yagia:

Can you tell me about what happened on the 27th of February last year?

Andie:

I was painting out the back; it was the last room that we had worked on. We had renovated the whole house, and we just finished the last room. Nick said, "It's going to flood tonight." We live in a raised house, so we moved everything upstairs. We had a knock on the door in the night. It was the SES asking, "Do you know it's going to flood? It'll be about the same as 2017." I thought that would be ok, we've been through floods before. So we took our cars up the hill. We tried to get some sleep, but too much was going on. My sense of time that night was way off. We got up and just watched the water rising. When it got to the top step, I thought, 'I wonder if Finny, our neighbour, knows.'

I called her and said, "Finny, is there water coming inside your house?" She looked down from her bed and said, "It's under my bed. What do I do?" and started to panic. She was on her own, with her two cats.

From then on, we were constantly on the phone to SES and the police, trying to get someone to rescue her. We found out later that she was on the phone with her dad for four hours as the water was rising, and she was standing on tables and chairs and getting her head closer and closer to the ceiling. Her dad thought she was going to die. We got word at 7 am that there was no help coming from emergency services. They told her she was on her own.

Finny's autistic. That call was too much for her. She didn't know how to cope, and she was saying, "I'll just come out of my house and swim to your house". But what she couldn't grasp at the time was that the water was flowing so fast, and there was so much stuff in it, if she made it out of her door, she would have died; she wouldn't have made it to our house, even though it's just next door.

In the 2017 flood, the water was slow and calm, and the rain was kind of drizzly, but this time it was torrential. The river that was flowing in the street was intense. Really intense. Finny did try to get out of her house, but she wasn't able to because the force of the water against the door was too much. So eventually our other neighbour knew someone who had a boat. After rescuing their own kids, they came back and got Finny.

It was just insane because it was the last minute that they could've been able to get her, as the water was about to go over the top of the doors and windows. If that had happened, they wouldn't have been able to find where to get into the house. They had to smash the glass in the back door and then drag her, bleeding, over the broken glass. And while they were dragging her out, their boat almost capsized.

For several hours, our entire focus was on what's going on next door. Trying to find somebody to get her help, talking to her to try and keep her calm. Just as they pulled her out, our smoke alarm went off. The gas pipe had snapped, and gas entered our entire house. I didn't realise that as I was leaning out the window trying to direct the boat, I was leaning over the gas leak. The exposure made me quite sick. I screamed at my family to go onto the veranda and wait for a boat to rescue us. It was a pretty traumatic experience. From the veranda, we could see a house on fire. I started panicking.

When a boat finally came for us, we had to leave our pets. I was very confused. The emergency and the stress of it all, plus the gas that I had been exposed to. I didn't have any kind of clarity. It was all very surreal to me, and having to leave the pets was just awful. But they were in their own survival mode.

The boat dropped us off at the Ballina Rd Bridge. From there, the kids got in a boat, and we got a ride on a jet ski to a safe drop-off point. When we got there, we already had some friends who had organised a place for us to go, which was just incredible, and our neighbour, Finny, came with us. I felt really blessed that everybody was providing food and clothes and all the things that we needed. We hadn't slept all night, and we were confused and exhausted.

Nick:

The next day I borrowed a canoe to get the pets. I couldn't get into Finny's to rescue her cats, but they survived. We belong to the Seventh-day Adventist church in Alstonville, and they reached out to help us. When we settled down from the emergency, we went into shock. We just went quiet and ate and slept. Andy got herself together and thought about renting somewhere for a while. We stayed in a farm shed until we could move in. It was horrible. Damp, mouldy, and a bare tin roof that was so loud when it rained. And it rained for six months after the flood.

The church gave us emergency money, food, and bedding, and our house was insured, so we knew that we'd be ok in the long run. Many of the older church members cooked for the flood refugees, and the church hall filled up with donations. They brought in washing machines for everyone to use, and even came into town to help with the cleanup. They organised themselves into teams for all the different tasks. Some took food and other items to places that were further out, like Wardell and Coraki, and others went out to help at the evacuation centers. And then, as time went on, the church identified some individuals needing help. They first focused on teachers and students from the Blue Hills school in Goonellabah, and organised grants and ongoing support to those people, as well as following up with them after a time to see how things are going.

We've found in the community that there are people who don't know what to do, and they're very confused. They don't have the money to do things, and just don't know what they should do. After the trauma and the clean-up, the uncertainty has sucked out their motivation. I guess we have insurance and renovation experience, and we refused to have our beautiful old timber lining boards and architraves ripped out by the insurance company, like what happened to so many affected houses, and we have each other to bounce off.

When I wanted to zone off under the doona, Andie would say, "Let's go, let's get into action." There was a lot of stuff to organise. Centrelink, insurance, rent, and school. After we cleaned up and the adrenaline rush settled, it hit me. I still get emotional when I think of all our stuff in a wet pile on the side of the road. I know it seems silly, but I miss my big fish tank, and Andie and I still go to get something, and then remember that it was lost in the flood. In hindsight, we should've saved certain things, and for a long time, the insurance company wouldn't help. It took nine months before we had a proper mattress to sleep on. The kids were with relatives while we sorted it out.

Yagia:

How has the flood experience affected you?

Nick;

I initially adopted a philosophy that the flood cleaned out our lives for a fresh start. Before the flood, my faith in Jesus was already growing as I was emerging from being a drug and alcohol addict. By the time the flood hit, I had cemented Jesus as being the way to change my life and become someone who serves others. I decided to look at the flood disaster as a way of service. I wanted to change my life. I feel I have met someone that I thought, Wow, this life is so much better with him, but I've still got all this stuff, and the message of Jesus is to serve others, not to serve myself. So I looked at it as, for a while, I'm free from commitments, so now I can serve others. Since then, we've both got more involved in our church. We both have ministries and run groups. So, I got a lot of comfort and help from my faith, although I'm still up and down, I'm still a bit traumatised.

Andie:

I'm glad the church gave us roles that we could go and help others. That helped me to focus outside of my own predicament. I'm the health ministry's team leader now, so I help run programs that help people with addictions, or smoking, or mental health issues, and that's giving me this greater sense of purpose in life.

You know, I float around what my purpose is. What's life all about? Why are we even here? And I think it wasn't necessarily because the flood happened. I think it was because I was a bit traumatised, and I didn't know what to do. When I was offered these positions to help people, I just went, "Yep, I'll do it", because I just didn't know what else to do. I couldn't figure out how to put the steps together to see where I wanted my life to go. Saying "Yes" to things has made my faith grow, because I can see now that I have a purpose, and that life isn't just about me. If life is just about me, what's the point?

Yagia:

Any closing comments?

Nick:

I love the community spirit that's been around. Initially, there was a lot of mismanagement from the government and insurance companies. I feel that when a disaster happens, you get the good and the bad. Luckily, our house wasn't too structurally damaged; it was more just the stuff inside our house that was destroyed.

Andie:

Nick's been working at half his pay rate to help people get back into their houses, and I've been helping people through the church. Yeah, we've kept ourselves really busy, and it's helped us process the grief and loss. Now, when I recall something lost in the flood, I have to have a moment of grief for it. It's still putting one foot in front of the other, but that's the process for moving forward.

CHAPTER 6
RAMA AND GRACE

❖

Rama

That day, we were going around town helping people. A lot of people knew the river would probably go over the wall and be a serious danger. I was sorting out work stuff and trying to get tools and machinery into different places. I wanted to keep my ute on the other side of town because I knew it would get locked in by the forthcoming flood.

I left it at my mate, Adil's, place on the other side of town, and asked him to move it if the water got that high, but when I got home. I realised I still had the keys. He rang me at 10 pm wanting to move it, as the water was rising. So I started out to his place.

It was a big mission. From home, I had to walk and wade all around the showground and North Lismore in the pouring rain to get there. I borrowed his kayak to get to where my ute was parked, then helped Adil move his stuff up from under his house.

Elyse, Adil's partner, said I'd be crazy to go home and offered me a bed. So I crashed out in the spare bedroom. I woke up an hour later to Elyse waking me up and saying, "It's bad, it's already under the house". As I was watching the rising water, my phone rang. My partner's sister and her family in South Lismore needed saving. I knew their house was quite high, which means there must be a lot of people in a bad situation. That's when it really hit me. This is bad.

I had this old tin boat at home that I had to get to, so I said goodbye to Adil and Elyse and set off. I left their place in the kayak about 4.30 in the morning, and it was pissing down so hard that I could hardly see, and it was dark. At one point, I remember when I was paddling into town, it felt like I was on a different planet. Around Woodlark Street, I heard screaming. The water was charging over the breakwall and powering down the street. I got to the service station. It was 5 am, and all the water around it was glistening with petrol. There was a big swell around a drain that leads to the pump station, then I saw what I thought was a log bobbing in the water. It was a man in trouble. I couldn't see that well, but I could hear the cry for help. I got to him, and he was able to grab onto the back of the kayak. When we got to Lismore Square, I asked him why he was in the water. He replied, "I woke up to it". He was homeless and sleeping on the street. I felt sad that someone in our society could be so vulnerable just because they were poor.

I kept heading back to my house to get the tinny. I thought I could make it to the bridge and walk home, but I got to Mary G's pub and there was no way. The water was so strong. The town was filling up, and the water had all sorts of stuff in it. I paddled around past Trinity school and got to the hill where the police station is. All the lights were on, so I knocked on the door to see what their plan was. There was no answer, and the door was locked. While there, I helped a woman nearby get out of her house, over her fence, and to safety. It was still dark, and I had to make it across the Richmond River. There were glowing things under the water, and I realised it was the street lights. This meant the electricity was still on. Then I looked up and saw that the main power lines were dipping into the water. The only way through was to go under them. Another danger to contend with.

I got to the bridge over the Richmond River, and there was a couple on the roof of that corner block of flats. As I was talking to them, an SES dinghy arrived, and I thought to myself, "Jeez, are we really in that sort of emergency?"

To cross the strong river current, I decided to go up the edge of the river and veer across as I came down with the current. When I got home, it was dawn. I had a cuppa and talked to my partner, Grace, about the mission. She had made the tinny accessible, as it was in a bad state from not being used for a year. I had a realisation about the intensity of what we were about to face. This wasn't just a big flood. The river changed direction. It was like picking up a suburb and dumping it in the open ocean.

We couldn't start the motor. Then Grace turned up with her spray–on deodorant, and it started. So the whole rescue depended on this can of deodorant. Grace was spotting, and I was driving the boat. We headed out towards North Lismore. When we got to Terania

Street, there were desperate people everywhere, constantly waving and screaming at us. We had to decide which house to go to.

The first house that we came to, the lady had two big suitcases with her. We were going in blind. There was no plan, no idea of what we do, or what we are capable of. What we soon realised was that people sitting on their roofs in the pouring rain were safe, and they were usually young and fit. So we decided to focus on families and older people, and those who couldn't climb onto their roof, either due to the design of the building, or the person's capability. We decided we would fill up the boat and drop people off at Nimbin Rd, near the cemetery, where the road starts to rise.

On our way to get Grace's sister, we kept coming across emergencies. People were screaming for us from everywhere. We probably would have been the first boat in that area, so we had to save people in dire straits first, but Grace knew her sister's kids were in the water waiting for us, and she was worried about them.

The big thing was crossing the raging river. We managed to avoid floating logs and then cross in front of the submerged bridge, which was very dangerous. If the motor had stalled, we would have slammed into it. It was incredibly stressful, and when we picked up families, we would often have to leave some of them behind.

Grace

We had to drop them off at the cemetery on Nimbin Road, where there is no shelter from the pouring rain, but there's only so much we could do; we had to hand it over. Later on, some people got airlifted to Dunoon, and some were ferried across town to Ballina Rd, then to the evacuation centre at the university.

We eventually got to my sister's place. The gutter was just a foot out of the water, and they were all clinging to it. It was 8.30 in the morning, and they had been like that for hours. We took them back to our place. Rama's dad was there. He was worried about us, and he took care of everyone. We got the kids in the shower, sat down, and had a chat about it. We knew we had to get back in the boat and keep going. I didn't want to, but I knew I had to. Three nights later, when everything had calmed down, we lay in bed, stared at the ceiling, and talked about it. We figure we saved close to 50 people and lots of pets.

We later bumped into an elderly couple at the Armistead photo exhibition that we had saved. When I saw them, I broke down and cried. In the flood, they were standing on furniture up to their shoulders and were literally saying their last words. These are old people. They can't endure this. And then we had to get them into the boat. I had to wrench these 80-year-old people into the boat and try not to hurt them. There was one larger lady we came across whose kids had gone in another boat. There was no way we could get her into the boat. We found furniture she could use, but she was worried she would be too much weight for the boat. Everything was difficult. Her legs were hurting from standing in the water for hours. Then she turned to me and said, "It's Ok, I've always known I'm a big girl. You guys can go now." We said, "No, we're getting you out of here." We finally found something for her to float on. When we got home, I broke down and cried. It was really tough. By 11 o'clock or 12 o'clock, lots of boats arrived, and we thought "Yes, it's going to be OK." By that time, the SES had started coordinating the rescue and sending boats to where they were needed. By 2 pm, we decided to go home. I stayed home, and Rama went back to help.

Rama

I started ferrying people, but then I ran out of fuel in the middle of the river. I got one of the passengers to hold onto a tree while I tilted the tank, then had to take them back to the Nimbin Rd drop-off point. I made my way towards home, but I ran out of fuel and pulled my way to safety with a power line. A police boat emerged from the distance and towed me home. Then I collapsed into bed.

It was such an intense experience. It's amazing what a strong community it is in South and North Lismore, how strong a people they are. I'd really like to see better preparation. Internal ladders to the roof, pontoons, and better rescue systems. The experience has built a community in me. I feel tied to the community, having shared the grief, trauma, and bravery of it. It seems crazy, but I feel like it's become part of who I am. It's not a linear story.

Grace

We went through so many emotions afterwards. We were angry that it was a forced civilian rescue and traumatic for so many people. Why wasn't the Army called in? We had no plan, no safety net, but we had to act. It's been a life-changing experience. Going through something like that puts everything into perspective. Life's values. Things that were important before aren't that important. Emotionally and pragmatically, I've had to re-assess my life.

CHAPTER 7
KRISTAL AND KAT.
DRAGONFLY CAFÉ

Kristal:

I decided to stay home that evening. We had learnt that the 1974 flood didn't come into our home in South Lismore, so we decided to stay, in the hope that we could save our things by raising them. We left our children with friends.

I was at work, and I remember hearing all the sirens and commotion around town. It was 4:30 in the afternoon. When I got home, it was on the news that a man had been found dead on Urallba Street. I intuitively thought about my dad, because the body was found near where he would park his car.

That night, I was feeling uneasy because the rain was so intense. I went to sleep at midnight and was woken two hours later by something knocking on the wall outside. The water had come into the house up to my knees. My ex-partner started to pick things up, and I thought, "That's not going to help". There was electricity in the water, so I suggested we go onto the veranda, where it was safe. When the water rose further, we managed to climb onto the roof, where we waited, shivering in the pouring rain for four hours until we got rescued by a couple of guys in a tinny. I was so frightened.

There were rescues happening on the whole street. We were dropped off at the old Norco building, because the tinny was too small to cross the raging river. Vince and Johnny were there with jackets and food. It was really nice to feel warm and fed, but I was beside myself with worry about my dad. Then the SES guys came a couple of hours later and ferried us through town to the Bruxner Highway drop-off point. We happened to have parked our cars near there when we moved them to higher ground, so we were able to drive straight to my boss's place in Goonellabah. Kat was also housing the families of other staff members.

I managed to keep my phone dry and called my mum to tell her I'm safe, then I got a call from my sister asking if I had heard from dad. No one had heard from him. I was very close to him and was worried. My sister put up a public post and a lot of people helped in the search, going to recovery centres, the hospitals, and the police. By Tuesday night, I was getting the feeling that my dad was the person reported on the news. It was a massive fear, and then on Wednesday, we were given the contact of a police officer who may know something about the body found in the drainpipe near the cinema.

We had to identify Dad through his jewellery and tattoos. His body was disfigured by being in water for three days, and we were advised that seeing him like that would be too traumatic. I was in complete shock. We all broke down and became very emotional. I think I was in complete shock for three months; it's all a haze. My dad was helping carry sandbags at the Golan hotel when he was swept into a drain pipe by the floodwater and released fifty meters away.

I spent two months with my sister and mother grieving over dad, then stayed with Kat for a couple of months. About June, the time Lismore council put on the concert at the showground for flood victims, I took up an offer from a friend who was leaving her apartment, and I'm still there with my two sons. My elder boy is at TAFE now. The flood ordeal has changed him. It's one positive that has come out of this. I've seen him change from being a typical fourteen-year-old teenager immersed in himself to being an aware, empathetic, passionate, thoughtful young man with direction in his life.

Now, when I'm not working at the café, I've recovered my interest in acting and am in a play called 'The Hungry Ghost', about addiction and the struggles in life. My dad used to love seeing me on stage, and I feel it's a way of connecting with him. Over the last year, I've learnt how to be vulnerable and allow myself to receive the love and support on offer. Emotionally, financially, or just in the friendship of connection, it's been very eye-opening for me to receive the support I've been given. As a mum, I'm used to being the supporter, and have had to shift to realise how giving and loving life is if you allow it. I love working at the café; we are such a family. We've all been through this together.

Kat:

2022 foods, 28 February. Up to 26 February, I thought I'd worked out the hospitality game. We'd got through Covid, and the masks came off on the Friday. There were smiles and joy, but it only lasted two days. I thought Covid was bad, but what happened in the flood, well, there are no words for it. Amongst all the things that happened in the flood, losing homes, losing dads, I wasn't aware that I was in shock until it hit me at the beginning of this year. I kept telling myself, "No, I'm not affected." I keep it positive for the staff; they don't need to see me upset. It's always better to find that ray of sunshine than be absorbed in darkness.

When I came downtown after the flood and stood at the door with all the mud and carnage and smell, I said to myself, "What do I do now? I've got nothing, nothing left." I had to decide whether to keep going or throw my hands in the air and say, "I can't do this." But I have such wonderful staff who need jobs and money, and homes and all sorts of things, so "Let's clean it up." We had to fix the whole building by ourselves. We cleaned and cleaned.

I had the target of opening by Anzac Day. We set up a gazebo tent in the shop to serve coffee and cordoned off the rest of the area. There was no ceiling or walls.   The dining floor survived, we got an insurance payout for the kitchen floor, and we saved two fridges. Now the walls are fibro, and the plan for another flood is to take everything to my garage. The government money has helped, but we've had to earn money to get money, and after Covid, there was nothing in the coffers. My saving grace was that I didn't have a mortgage and was able to get a loan to get the business going, and the building owner wanted us back. We've slowly but surely come back, and I'm grateful for my staff and the community. It took over a year to get the building repaired, which was going on while we were in business.

There was a lovely lady called Terrie who came and planted flowers, and lots of our customers and strangers came and helped in the clean-up. My son and his friend came down from Brisbane, and there were even people from the Gold Coast who would come down and offer petrol, generators, and pressure cleaners. The fire brigade was awesome. I'd put in for a couple of jobs for the Army when they were here, but I had leaking pipes and things that couldn't wait.

All the staff were amazing, they all put in a magnificent effort. We started back with a generator and three power points. Too many lights would trip it and turn off the coffee machine. Over time and patience, we gradually came back, and the community has continued to support us. That's why I brought my lounge from home. The café has been a meeting place. Lots of laughter and tears. They've had experience of loss too, and understood what we were going through. Under terrible conditions for my staff, we provided a space for everyone. Our community is so unique. It's diverse and supportive, and we all pull together and help each other.

We've come through this. I love this town, I love the people. I'm honoured that people respect what we do here, because it's about community. It's not all about me or money. The town hasn't got a lot of money after the flood. I decorate the café with beautiful staff and good food. As Kristal's dad used to say, "Onwards and upwards, never above you, never behind you. Always beside you."

CHAPTER 8
JANELLE SAFFIN
NSW PARLIAMENT

I want to step back to 2017. That was the biggest flood we knew of in recorded history, although there might have been others before white settlement.

Not much was done after then, and I was not in parliament at that time, and I wasn't thinking of coming back. I decided not to comment on issues and let the respective members do their thing. After the 2017 flood, I wrote a letter saying that they should've called for category D funding. Category D means you get a declaration of catastrophic, and then other things flow. Not much happened in response.

So I ran for parliament again, and when I got elected, I asked each local government body what their mitigation plans were around adaptation, so that I could start to advocate for change. However, immediately after I got elected, we had the big bushfires, and I went straight into working with people in the Tenterfield community.

Then there was drought, the mice plague, Covid, and then the mega flood of 2022, which I called a humanitarian disaster. I use that term because we think that only happens overseas, but not in our own backyard. I also use the term 'internally displaced people', which is usually in the context of refugees from a war zone or major overseas disaster, but that's what's happened to us.

The weekend of the flood, February 2022, I was having meetings with SES and others at the highest level about what might be coming. I was hearing from locals as well as people I know who have some expertise in weather that something big was coming. I didn't see any preparedness, a readiness, even when I asked about what warnings were to be announced.

I live by the river, and always stay in town when floods happen, because I can then access and arrange services and keep working. Our place always gets cut off, but never floods inside. So I came into town and stayed with friends in Cathcart Street, in a place that had never flooded before.

In the morning, we swam out of the house because the water was rising. I was aware during the night that the people were reaching out for help, that emergency services were not answering when you rang the SES or 000. I get that there were thousands of calls, but there's a thing in emergency services that if the system becomes overloaded, calls can be diverted to other services such as Voluntary Rescue Australia, Marine Rescue, Foreign Rescue, RFS, all of that. Calls could have been patched through, and they weren't. That shows me something that needs to change. Also, that night, I was acutely aware that people were saying goodbye to their loved ones. I knew this from Facebook and the calls I was getting.

We've had a physical disaster, but this was also a humanitarian disaster, and that has many dimensions to it. The trauma shapes what happens for some time, for individuals and the community. I still see that bureaucracies in Sydney and Canberra haven't realised this.

Going back to the house in Cathcart Street. I didn't sleep that night. A colleague rang and told me to get my husband, Jim, out of the house. I replied, "I think it's too late", and I knew Jim would not leave our dog behind. Because there was no warning, we were a bit complaisant, then my friend rang back and told us to leave where I was staying.

I woke up my friends, Susan and Marg. It was 2 am, and we could hear voices and banging through the sound of pouring rain. We rang the SES as a local in trouble. The woman was lovely and suggested putting chairs on the table to get out of the water. I remember Marg looking at us and saying, "Are you stupid? That's not going to work, you'll be sitting ducks, we have to get out." So we stood on the verandah railing, and the water kept coming. I was on the phone with my husband and my neighbours. We realised there was no help coming. Through my fog of emotions, I remember ringing Walt, one of my parliament colleagues, and telling him that I don't think we will get out of here.

In the light of dawn, a helicopter appeared. Everybody in the street was waving for help. The three of us jumped off the verandah rail and started swimming up Cathcart Street. We avoided a dangerous patch and headed towards a tire that was stuck in a tree. Then Harry, my staff member who lives nearby, came from around the corner in a lime green inflatable canoe. He heard me calling, but I wasn't calling for help; I was singing out to a couple of neighbours who were trapped. I was ok. I trained as a lifesaver in my early days, and I knew how to read the water. I said, "Harry, go and save those people first," then I thought, "Shit, I don't know how capable he is, I don't even know if he can swim." He managed to get her out, even after the canoe upturned.

Then there was another neighbour, Bernie, who was stuck. I found a wooden plank and tried to get him out using that, but it didn't work. Then another fellow came up from Park St. in a canoe. I screamed at him to come down, and Bernie was saved.

By then, I thought my husband had drowned. I had to stay focused. I had to put that thought aside and get to work. I thought that as the local member, I had to work to bring attention to this disaster. We canoed and walked up the hill to Harry's mum's place, and I went to work contacting the media, agencies, and anyone who could help. I was aware that locals were out in the water rescuing each other. One local media outlet had been called by SES to take their post down that encouraged locals to take their boats out to save people. I replied, "Do you want people to live?" he said, "Of course I do". I replied. "Then ignore the directions from the SES, and I will back you up". I was aware there was a tiny army growing and the different orders they were getting. At one stage, while on the phone, I watched a Blackhawk helicopter rescue two people I know from their roof. I had managed to save my phone, and people were ringing me constantly. It was a case of linking people with services where possible.

Through the night, I was also in touch with my neighbours, who have a studio for the Hussy Hicks band. I basically said, "No one is coming, there is no SES, there's nothing."

They have an old canoe, and they knew Jim was at home. At some point in the night Jules crossed the river and managed to get him out, and then held him until daylight, when they were both saved by another canoe.

Everyone woke to what was needed. The emergency service at Southern Cross University got going because they had done it before. It was literally the vice chancellor and the deputy vice chancellor who kicked it off. It happened across the region. At Xavier School in Ballina, too, everybody was just doing what they could. As Aidan Ricketts said, "We had complete anarchy for a couple of weeks, and it worked".

I was on the phone with everyone. The premier, the opposition, the federal government, and the various services, saying, "What's happening? Who's coming? How are we going to deal with this? We need fuel, we need food." An example was when I was talking to Essential Energy because power had gone down at Lismore Base Hospital. The generators kicked in, but they needed fuel. When that was sorted, I rang them back and said we've got St Vincent's Hospital too. I told them that although it's a private hospital, it backs up the public system. So they got power happening there, too.

Now it's been almost two years since the flood. I feel that the lack of preparedness and the lack of a government body capable of preparing and responding still needs work. The community has been absolutely remarkable. We're still in recovery, but we're also doing a major adaptation plan of a Resilient Lands Program and a Resilient Homes Program. It's messy. I work on it daily. But, you know, it's never been done before, and never designed like that. So we're doing these two things at once. That adaptation should've happened years back, so we've got to do it now. But we're doing that at the same time that we're doing recovery.

Businesswise, people have been remarkable and stepped up everywhere. In this region, business and community are all merged together, and that's a good thing, because we need a functioning economy and a functioning community. The one thing that's missing, that I called for from day one, was, I said, "This is our Tracy moment." Referring to the 1974 hurricane that decimated Darwin. I know older people remember Tracy. I said this is our 'Tracy' moment. We need a comprehensive, wraparound, economic, environmental plan that covers the spectrum of issues. To me, this has been the one missing element all the way through.

It's being worked on, but we have discussions like: "Is it too late? Is it still viable?" A whole lot of things have rolled out anyway, so how do we integrate everything into a working system? I've just got someone in a position of Regional Coordinator for the delivery of services. We didn't have that before. A go-to person. Plus a few other positions like that. All of the services have stepped up to the challenge, like the local Neighbourhood Centres, and the local businesses everywhere. They have been fantastic. What they did, and what they donated.

We didn't have a plan. Even sketched on a whiteboard. It would have really helped to have a plan. Even now, local government is still after that. So I've got what I call a 'Community Driven 'plan that's being worked on. Community drives and articulates the needs, and then we have conversations with all the people who can support that. You don't get everything you want, but it's in the right direction. Resilient Lismore is one example.

The Two Rooms project they started, which started with Ellie Bird. It's now got Joel Jensen constructions. He jumped on board, working on a lot of voluntary stuff.

The Lismore Catholic Diocese saw the vision and stepped in. The Winsome emergency accommodation, Mountain Blueberries and nursery, Ian Phillips Good Food pantry, and others. They've all come together. They were all running on donations. I just secured five million dollars out of the budget to allow them to continue their work. It was funny. When they all came to Sydney to meet with the premier, they said, "Yeah, we want the money, but we don't want to be tied up in red tape." So they organised a system where they're only accountable to each other.

I strongly felt that I could push for change. I advocated for a New South Wales Reconstruction Authority, similar to the Queensland Reconstruction Authority. We didn't have anything like that. They do a state mitigation plan where they work with local councils and local communities to develop their own adaptation plans. Recognition of mitigation and adaptation to climate change is built into the legislation, amongst other things I've advocated for. I was in the opposition party at the time, but I got the government of the time to agree. Although the existing Northern Rivers Reconstruction Corporation did a few good things and brought money into the plan, their ideas were badly implemented. The new body sped up repairs of roads and bridges and invested in cultural arts projects, pod villages, land for a tradie's site, a smooth flow for buy-backs, and those sorts of things.

I recognised that healing in the community could not be done by grants alone. Historically, that's what happens, but we need more than a grant-led recovery. The Northern Rivers Reconstruction Corporation was woeful with communication.

Traditionally, government agencies don't like to go out into the community and say things, unless they've already ticked all the boxes. This situation was not like that. We need the fluidity of people talking to people. Resilient Lismore is like that. Ellie is doing a great job. I really wanted government people to go into the community, but it didn't happen. After the Queensland flood, they door-knocked 18,000 homes to see how they could help. Now we're doing that. Just as well, too. Some people have said they never would've reached out for mental health support, grants, and Centrelink support. It's not going to fix everything, but it's saying 'We're here,' And we've all got to be sensitive and trauma-informed. For example, I recently looked at a letter that was about to be sent out, and I said, "No, no, you can't use that language with someone who sat in a ceiling, trapped with the kids for hours, saying goodbye to them."

Our community is amazing. They've shown absolute strength and innovation in how they have responded. I get how hard this has been. It's certainly been hard for me, separating the personal from the public. My driving force has always been public advocacy and trying to ensure our community is able to recover and thrive.

I see the whole recovery like a mosaic. It's not linear. It's so many things happening at once. Ideally, we would have these plans worked out without the recovery happening at the same time.

CHAPTER 9
NAOMI MORAN,
KOORI MAIL NEWSPAPER

The Koori Mail has been here for over twenty years, so we've seen some floods, but the level of water this time was something we'd never seen before. On the Sunday of the flood, I was on the Gold Coast spending some time with a good friend of mine. My husband was messaging me saying, 'It's getting worse, I think you should come back down,' so I rushed down.

I came into the office at about 5 o'clock that afternoon with my husband, our kids, and some friends of his from Fiji, and together with some of our staff, we elevated things to the top of the tables.

Printers, computers, documents – things that were important to stay operational. When we left, we thought it would be okay. The information we were receiving at the time was around 12 metres.

A few hours later, the predictions were that this was going to be the biggest flood we've ever seen. Around about midnight, we went back into the CBD. We had about an hour to consider what we could do. In panic mode, we had to decide what we could save. We foolishly pushed lots of things into the podcasting room and hoped for the best. Thankfully, we got all our computers and our hard drives out. At that point, I kind of waved a white flag and said, 'Anything else that goes under, so be it.' We didn't have the time or the manpower to raise anything else.

When we got home in the early hours of that morning, we were constantly looking on social media to see what the updates were. I was holding my breath to see what was happening, how much water had come in, and when the levee would break. It was like watching a slow death.

When I saw footage of the building, I had a sinking feeling. I knew whatever we had downstairs was gone. 30 years of archived print editions of the Koori Mail are completely inundated. Important documents. Really important and special artworks that the Koori Mail has collected over the years. There was even an original Albert Namatjira floating around; we have no idea where it went.

I started at the Koori Mail when I was 14 years old, so I took it personally. When you're in a position of leadership, it hits hard because the reality of it is that I'm responsible now.

Also, as a Bundjalung person, there is a responsibility for an entire group that will look to this organisation for help. People are looking for support in probably one of the most traumatic times in their lives. So, all of this was going through my mind when I saw footage on TV and in the days that followed. I knew intuitively that the hit of water had devastated the whole community. I sent a text message to every single person in my contact book. Everyone from prominent Aboriginal leaders to Indigenous football players. I sent the same message saying, 'We need your help.'

The hubs were something we'd never done before. I still can't explain how it happened. I remember saying, "We just need to do this". We set up a big tent, one table, and a couple of signs. "Drop food off here". "Help us". It snowballed into something bigger than what we could have ever imagined.

I strongly feel that the Koori Mail, contributing to the Australian and Indigenous media landscape for over 30 years, has bolstered the support that we needed for this community. Droves of volunteers started coming in from everywhere. The key volunteer group that we had was the Bundjalung mob. They were the organisational and driving force of the flood hub. Others stepped into volunteering because they respected them, and they valued them, and they trusted the Koori Mail. We needed the voices of those who have been traumatised by this event. Those who lost everything. That's when the help started coming in. Droves of volunteers came to help. Our wonderful local Bundjalung women were the driving force, and people respect them.

Sending that text message out was a risk. Maybe only one person would reply. Asking people for help is never an easy thing. I was putting the reputation of the Koori Mail on the line. The hub became huge. Free clothes and bedding, free counselling and medical, free food, and someone to talk to, and something to do. Some people thought the hub was just for blackfells. No, we're part of the community, and this is us supporting the whole community. Of course, we created a culturally safe space. We even had some elders here for the mob to talk with, but we had people from everywhere come to help and be helped.

What we started with was to form relationships with philanthropic groups and retailers in our region to provide essentials. We set up what we fondly called the Koori Coles. Everything from bedding to band aids. We had signs that showed you where your pasta, your rice, and your dog food were. People could come in and do a grocery shop and stay for a meal from the Koori Kitchen. Everything was donated, everything was for the community. The first floor of our building was cleaned out and set up with shelves to house all the donations from all over Australia. Aunty Rose and Auntie Monica organised it. People could come and take what they needed for free.

We had doctors in the area that were donating their time so people could come in and get triaged on the spot, and get their prescriptions refilled if their chemist was flooded, so we set up a medical tent. We had medical people working with diabetics and kidney dialysis, and a space for the volunteer masseurs, counsellors, and psychologists to work. The doctor would treat an infected cut from the floodwater and refer them to counselling if they emotionally broke down. When it comes to caring for people in the most traumatic time of their lives, it's important to take a holistic approach. It's not just about getting food, water, clothing, and a hot meal to take away. It's making sure that emotionally and mentally, you're being supported as well.

We had some special space for our elders to come along so that our local mob could get that Nan and Pop kind of love that is so invaluable in a cultural context for us. Some of our elders would just come in and sit there with a cup of tea all day, every day. They weren't flood-affected, but they knew that this was where they had to be. For many, they were the still, guiding light amongst all the chaos. Then we had these key groups of men from our community. Bundjalung men who stood by our side for the whole time. They coordinated things like helicopter drops to Tabulum and Box Ridge. Somebody rang us and asked if we could use their helicopter. Our volunteers would meet them with the boxes to deliver. Others offered their boats, jet skis, trucks, commercial fridges, and generators. It was all coordinated by these amazing men. There was no help from the government, the army, or even NGO's. It was all community-driven. Our mob is used to working like that. It was that spirit of warriors and caregivers that was common before colonisation.

Then, of course, there was the fundraising. We originally set out to generate $100,000. We raised over $1.3 million. It was a big responsibility and absolutely something that we'd never done before. We were aware of scams. What we decided to do was make sure that we did it the right way. We made sure that people who were really flood-affected received that money. Local major businesses jumped on board. Harvey Norman, Good Guys, Buy Rite, and others. If you registered with us, you could then go to those retailers. They would send their invoices to us, and we would pay with that fundraising money. Some government money went into the people's bank accounts, but we wanted to make sure they could get what they needed. We reached out to our Indigenous organisations that were affected by the flood as well. Everyone from our local foster care agencies to the Cabbage Tree Island school received a portion of those funds.

The Koori Mail had to stop printing for the first time in 30 years. We had to support the community first. The fact that we've only just started rebuilding downstairs, 12 months later, is a testament to that. My day job has well and truly returned now, but we're also coming through with some really exciting times for the space downstairs. How do we take all of the good stuff from last year that connected our communities? How do we continue that? How do we take the days of Aunty Tanya doing weaving and cultural therapies day after day and present their vibe in our space? So, downstairs we're building a coffee shop and an event space where people can come in for workshops, yarning sessions, the local footy presentation, whatever it is. A space for people to feel strong and connected to who they are.

People would ask me, 'How do you do it? Are you okay?' I joke that for the past 12 months, I was running on coffee, adrenaline, and the odd margarita. But honestly, it's important to me that the work that we're doing honours the work of those who have come before us. That's the difference in how genuine your approach is to serve your community. As an Aboriginal organisation, we never stop serving our community. It's not something we hang up and put on the next day like a raincoat, depending on the weather. I'm very passionate about the foundations of who I am as a First Nations person, as a Bundjalung person, and a Nyanganbal Dungutti person. There's a lot of responsibility that comes with that. And my job roles into my identity. Yes, the Koori Mail Hub was exhausting and tiring, and I had my moments where I was like, 'How am I going to do this?' There were times I would go home, and when nobody could see me, I would have my moments. But part of the leadership that a lot of us feel, as Aboriginal and Torres Strait Islander people, is that we are gifted by those who came before us. We have to tap into that cultural strength and give time to our emotions after the work is done. We draw on the strength of, well, we've only been doing it for 60 thousand years, right?

So, I reflected on those who had come before us and the history of this nation. I reflected on people like my grandfather, who was taken from Cabbage Tree Island at age 9 and sent to the Kinchela Boys Home. He no longer had his name, Edward Moran, but he was given a number, number 701. These are the things that I start to think about when I'm facing a challenge. When I'm going, 'Holy shit, how am I going to keep my staff in a job? Who am I going to ask for help?' You know, during those times, you might feel like you don't have the answers, but you'll find them if you really think about what it was like for the people who came before us. They had no choice but to find an answer. 'How am I going to survive ten whole years away from my mother and father before I can return to Cabbage Tree Island?' He was taken at nine and returned as a nineteen-year-old. So, for me, getting up at five o'clock in the morning and not going to sleep until 1 am after a day's work, and trying to be a mum and a wife and everything in between, I kinda go, hey, that's nothing. I'm a big believer that everything that I've been able to do and achieve is only possible because of those old fellas. Now we have a group of people that can say, 'We wouldn't have been able to rebuild if it wasn't for the Koori Mail.' That's what I mean by cultural responsibility.

Our response was a really good example of breaking down the mentality that Aboriginal people cannot self-determine their own affairs. To be labelled the rebellious one, or the trouble-maker, because we decided to pitch a big old tent in the carpark … well, I'm sorry, but I'm not being disrespectful by not lodging a council application to pitch a tent, what I'm actually doing is acknowledging that people come first. The labels that mean more to me are the ones that come from my community. My elders, my family, and my staff members. They're the ones that go, "Right, she did well."

Those other labels almost affected me to the point where I may not have gotten up one day. Unfortunately, it's a real reflection of some individuals in the community who don't know a world where blackfellas control their own affairs. It scares them. They're more comfortable with White Australia controlling everything. Their prejudices blind them. What we did was for everybody. We made sure that we provided a culturally safe space, not just for our own mob to come and get help, but for non-Indigenous people in this community as well. For them to come to an Aboriginal-owned and occupied space and feel comfortable was a special thing.

I feel like everything that I do every day now is healing me. I'm learning, listening, and understanding. So I'll take that, thank you, and I'll keep doing what I need to do to support all of my community. Whether it's a flood, whether it's recovery or politics, whatever it is.

CHAPTER 10
SATNAM
MASALA FUSION RESTAURANT

In the aftermath of the 2022 Lismore flood, I walked into Satnam's restaurant as one of the volunteers wandering around to see who needed help. The place looked like a bomb had hit it. There was a brown mud wash on everything. The walls and ceiling were peeling. Chairs and tables were lying amongst broken glass, and the silence of tragedy wafted through everything. Stacks of bottles were on a table in a vain effort to create a semblance of order, and standing alone in the middle of all this was Satnam. He turned with a smile to greet me, as he knew me as one of his customers, but soon into the conversation, his despair and overwhelming trauma showed themselves. He held back tears as he told me his fear of his family becoming homeless, as he had bought the building only three months before the flood, using his house as security on the loan, and now there was no income and little prospect of repairing the restaurant. Ten minutes later, a woman turned up and announced that her husband and ten of his mates would arrive to help clean up. That was the turning point. Like so many Lismore locals that metamorphose into angels when called to help, these tradie-looking guys worked all day for free. I think it was the first time Satnam felt supported, but he's a cook, not a builder. From there, it was a case of turning the Titanic around.

Satnam:

I came to Australia in 2007 to study hospitality. My family business in the Punjab is in restaurants, so I have been working in hospitality since my childhood. After connecting with the Sikh community in Melbourne, I met a wonderful Australian girl. A few years later, we married and moved up this way to start a family. My first job here was with Henry's bakery, just up the road. We saved enough to start an Indian restaurant in Byron Bay, 'Bombay to Byron', which is still running. From there, we settled back in Lismore, and in 2018, we opened the Masala Fusion restaurant, which was going really well until the flood hit. As everyone knows, it was a huge blow to every business in town. I lost about half a million dollars 'worth of equipment and stock, and I'm still dealing with the stress and trauma of the event.

When the warning came and the water was rising, we moved everything up, but it wasn't enough. At 1 a.m. that morning, I just made it out as the levee broke. When I came back to survey the damage, I had to crawl over the broken glass of a fridge that was blocking the entrance. A wall had collapsed, the ceiling had fallen, expansion from water stopped the doors and windows from opening, and the whole area was broken, messy, and smelled of mud. I was sad. I couldn't sleep for weeks, wondering what to do next. How could we come out of this? I figured the best way to start was to help others. I chose not to come to the restaurant for a while because it was too distressing. Some of my Sikh friends from Sikh Volunteers Australia came up from Melbourne, and we set up a kitchen at my house, making about 1,200 meals a day to give away. We were sending them to the distribution hubs around town. At that time, there was no food available for anyone. By the time my friends returned to Melbourne, the Koori Mail community hub had started in the carpark. I took my big commercial-size pots down there and asked if I could help. For the next few months, I split my time between working at the hub, cleaning up at the restaurant, and working as a security guard to pay the bills. The love and support I got from volunteering recharged me to face the devastating mess at my business. I think the Koori kitchen gave me more than I gave it. I made lots of good friends, and some of them helped me fix up the restaurant. Stella still helps out. I've never asked for help before, but with donations from my Go-Fund-Me page and some money from the government, I'm slowly getting back on my feet, although I still haven't had a holiday yet. My parents saved up and came out to support me, which is so touching. I am so grateful for all the help in getting my family back on our feet. The restaurant is almost back in full swing now. It's so nice to be back on board, and I'm so grateful for everyone who's helped out.

CHAPTER 11
THANH TRAN
MILLERS BAKERY

We took over ownership of businesses one month before the flood hit.

On Sunday, one day before the flooding, we had a note from the council to prepare and pack. Something like that. We didn't know about the flooding from 2017, so we just lifted our stuff onto tables. But the flooding was too big.

We unluckily. That day we had party with my aunty in Brisbane, so all my brother and sister go to Brisbane. It was only me and wife here. Lucky we had some people around here who help me lift cabinets, display fridges to put in my truck. Just someone who go around asking, 'Do you need help?' and we say 'Yes.'

Most of cabinets, oven and all machines to make dough and all stock go under dirty water.

When I saw news in morning I think it be really horrible. It really, really hard to say what my thinking were that morning.

In cleanup, so everything really messy. All glass doors broken. All rubbish come in from street, all way to back of shop. Rubbish bins through shop, the green ones, and red ones. Broken glass, everything.

We lucky, we had people from Gold Coast, people from everywhere come here help clean up. We had good friend from Wardell and Lismore who help clean. It took over ten days.

We born Vietnam. It take six hours from Ho Chi Minh city to Dak Lak province. I 24 year old when come to Australia. Now I 32.

I want come to Australia to live because I working hard and make money. In Vietnam it much harder. If you work hard one day you can buy just one kilo rice. It day-to-day surviving.

First time we come here we have to work in meat works. It OK. After four years meat company sponsor us, we got permanent residence.

My two brother, my sister, my parents, all living together here in Lismore and I moved here to live with them, to help.

It was first time in my life to see flooding like that. I never go through anything bad as that.

My parents, my brother all work here at bakery. My sister work in nail shop in Lismore Central shopping complex, but all shops go under water. so that's why we have no job for few months in Lismore.

We no insurance. Owner of building have insurance, but we own none for business. All cabinets we buy one month before flooding. We pay for baker's supply in Brisbane. Fifty-three thousand dollar. All brand new. All go under water. So after flooding we pay for twenty thousand dollar more to go fix and clean up again.

We had close for nine months here at Millers Bakery, waiting for landlord to fix flooring and electricity. We really lucky we have good landlord. If they not do anything it be really hard to come back again.

The other shop in East Lismore we not to do anything. We buy rolls and sweet cakes from Alstonville, we closed only two months and then come back to selling again. We try to keep customer coming back so support with debt.

We very lucky my parents loan me some money from my country to pay rent for the shop in the CBD for that time. Some staff they have to find another job in Brisbane, but we have big family in Lismore. My nephew, my niece, my brother, so they here for a short time after flood, working on lettuce farm in Wardell to make money, and after they come back here.

Before flooding, in this road it really busy, after the flooding too many business people are gone so it really hard for us now, because not many people go around here. Really hard financially, because we just bought house for family, and after that everything's going up. Rent on the shop, home loan, flood, it really horrible.

I work hard seven days. I here early for make bread. After work we get dinner. Then I go home to sleep. One good thing, it easy to go sleep (laughs).

We had some staff who worked in front, they move to Brisbane after flood, but my brother living in Tamworth working in meat processing. He come here to work with family.

I'm lucky we have our own bakery for my family. My nephew, my brother are bakers. All Vietnamese roll they learn from a guy from Vietnam, all the sweet cake he learn from TAFE.

We also have Vietnamese rolls and beef noodle soup, and Vietnamese coffee. The way we make it here is same one as how I learn make it in Vietnam. Vietnamese food really popular here. We want to offer more Vietnamese food for our customers. People in Lismore good people.

POSTSCRIPT

The government warning systems failed, but anyone who had been living in the area for a while could see that this was going to be a big one. The ground was already drenched. As the sky stayed black and the weather continued to demonstrate who's in charge, the creeks and rivers merged to form a huge lake, swallowing anything that dared try to stand against it. The systems failed in so many ways, but were often compensated for by a sensible and compassionate community. The emergency services refused to cross the river, so strangers in boats came to the rescue. The army came in late with a fanfare of politicians, showing how they have the cleanup under control. They repaired essential services, but it was the army of local young people who took up mops and pressure cleaners to clean strangers' houses. In the week after the flood, the internet and phones were down. Shops and petrol stations that survived had nothing because trucks couldn't get through, or they were underwater. Access to anything was difficult. Petrol, communications, food, generators, and cleaning products. Everything. Land slips caused house and road damage. Mt Nardi tower, essential for communication and part of Australia's defence network, became inaccessible. My neighbour went to relieve himself on the veranda in the early morning and thought he was dreaming while looking at the tree in front of him getting lower and then disappearing. The whole side of the mountain collapsed. The hills around Mullumbimby were especially affected.

The flood water and its residue were another problem. In Lismore, the floodwater was polluted with mud, chemicals, and animal waste. It rushed through farms that once had forests, causing water to speed and cause damage. The water was so toxic that any cut would get infected and turn septic. In Byron Bay and Ballina, the floodwater was cleaner.

Many businesses lost hundreds of thousands of dollars. Norco, the local dairy factory, managed to get a government grant of thirty million dollars for repairs and flood preparedness. The council got grants to repair infrastructure. The Lismore supermarket complex used the repairs to upgrade the building and the shopping presentation. They brought tradespeople from interstate as all the local trades were booked to capacity.

After the flood, nearly a thousand homes were never replaced. With residents displaced and often homeless many left the area and local businesses continued to struggle.

The government set up well-thought-out recovery methods. Lismore council put on a free concert by Paul Kelly to give some respite for the flood victims, and the NSW government created a designated body to make available individual plans and funds, including mental health counselling. They set up a buyback plan for many houses, where the owners get the pre-flood worth for their house as long as it is moved or destroyed. Small businesses got a $20,000 repair grant, and some put out a 'go-fund-me' page.

Now, three years after the flood, there are wire fences around many houses. A precursor to their disappearance, leaving many open spaces in the low area around the CBD. All the low areas have been hit with unrealistic insurance and building demands, leading to inhibitions in recovery to the way things were. Lismore is changing. The restrictions mean that the old buildings will stay, while the short distance to Byron Bay implies it will always have the motivation to be a great place to live. The council is trying.

They built a community bike trail and a great skate park in town, and are accommodating the changes in architecture, services, and people. Lismore will raise its head and shake off the water. Everyone is more alert now. It looked like it was going to flood in March 2025, and the services moved quickly in preparation. The community is forced to reconcile and adapt to nature, and does it well. For those who are left, the future looks promising.

Yagia Gentle